MONSTER ITCH

ITCH

GHOST ATTACK

MONSTER ITCH

ITCH

GHOST ATTACK

By David Lubar

Illustrated by Karl West

SCHOLASTIC INC.

This book is a work of fiction. Names, characters, places, and incidents are either the product of the author's imagination or are used fictitiously, and any resemblance to actual persons, living or dead, business establishments, events, or locales is entirely coincidental.

ISBN 978-0-545-87348-2

10 9 8 7 6 5 4 3 2 1   17 18 19 20 21

Printed in the U.S.A. 40

First printing 2017

Book design by Mary Claire Cruz

For Dr. Ronald Julia, Dr. Donald Schinstine,
Dr. Patrick Brogle, Dr. Joseph Trapasso,
and Dr. Marilyn McDonald.

Thank you for keeping me walking, smiling, seeing,
breathing, and all that good stuff. I am fortunate to
be in such talented, caring, and capable hands.

ONE

"You're killing me!" I screamed.

My shouts made the grip grow tighter. I struggled to breathe, but my ribs had no room to expand. "Let go."

"But I'll miss you so much, Alex," Mom said.

I glanced past her at Dad, who offered me nothing more helpful than a shrug. If shrugs could talk, this one would have said, *You're on your own.*

And right past Dad, my cousin Sarah, who had just gotten out of the car, also shrugged. But the message from her shoulders, as they brushed against the ends of her brown hair, was more like, *I'm glad your parents brought us here and not mine.*

I could understand how she felt. Both our moms loved hugs and hated good-byes.

"It's just for one week," I said, using the last air in my lungs.

That didn't help. As Mom clamped down, I could feel my belly button pressing against my backbone.

"For goodness' sakes," Grandma said, coming down the front-porch steps of her house. "Stop

trying to squeeze him in half. He's already enough of a handful to keep an eye on. There's no way I'll watch two of him— even if each one is just half the size."

Mom loosened her grip enough so I could escape.

"Hi, Grandma," I said. I spun a safe distance from Mom's arms. "We're here."

Grandma shot me a sharp look. If looks could talk, this one would have said, *Don't waste my time stating the obvious. Of course you're here.* But then the glare softened, and she said, "Glad you kids came for a visit. I can't wait for you to see the new place. Take your bags upstairs. There's a guest room at each end of the hall."

I inhaled a deep breath of the fresh country air, then walked over to the car.

"What a great house," Sarah said. "I'll bet it's haunted." She flashed me a grin.

Just because I didn't like creepy movies, she was always trying to scare me.

"That's why we bought it," Grandma said. "They promised there'd be a ghost. But I suspect they were trying to fool us city folks."

She's a writer. And Gramps is an artist. They make this comic book called *Little Grendella* about a girl who's a monster. It's really twisted, but not too scary for me.

Gramps joined Grandma on the porch and said, "The place is wonderfully creaky." He laughed and added, "Just like me."

He was joking. Grandma and Gramps are both in great shape. They go skiing and hiking all the time. They even own a pair of kayaks.

Sarah and I unhooked our bikes from the rack on the back bumper of the car and wheeled them over to the side of the garage. As we were walking back to the car, Dad popped the trunk. I reached in and grabbed my duffle bag.

That's when Grandma said, "One of the rooms is a teeny tiny bit nicer than the other."

She might as well have said, "On your mark. Get set. Go!"

Sarah and I ran flat out for the front door. Just because she's five whole days older than me, she always thinks she should get the first choice, the biggest piece, and the best seat.

Not this time. I might not be a faster runner than Sarah, but I was a lighter packer. My bag didn't slow me down at all, while hers was so heavy she almost had to drag it. I reached the steps with a good lead.

"Wait!" Mom shouted. "You forgot something!"

I looked back. That was a mistake, because I also kept running forward.

"Oof!"

I tripped on the bottom porch step. Luckily, the stairs broke my fall.

"I'm okay," I said, bouncing back to my feet before Mom could start checking me for wounds.

Sarah raced past me and flung open the screen door. Mom raced toward me, holding *THE BOX*. "You almost forgot this." She thrust it at me. I could hear footsteps upstairs as Sarah ran toward the right side of the second floor.

"Don't worry," Grandma said, snatching *THE BOX* from Mom. "I'll take good care of everything and everyone."

I used to have really bad allergies. That's why Mom had brought *THE BOX*—it was full of stuff to treat sneezes, wheezes, coughs, itches, twitches, and pretty much anything else that didn't need stitches. She was terrified that I'd get sick. The fact that she's a doctor doesn't help. The fact that she's an *allergy* doctor makes things a whole lot worse. I can't even scratch a tiny itch on my arm around her without getting cov- ered with creams, ointments, and lotions.

If she hears me cough or sneeze, I'm totally doomed to spend the rest of the day in bed, even if I feel fine.

Grandma told Mom not to worry in seven or eight more ways and finally got her heading back to the car. I heard Sarah run to the other end of the hall. Then the steps stopped. I guess she'd had plenty of time to look at each room and choose the best one for herself. Oh, well. It's not like the rooms would be all that different.

Mom reached the car. "Take care of yourself," she called.

"Bye." I gave my folks a last wave as they got into the car.

Last wave?

Yikes. That thought made my throat close up a little. As excited as I was to spend time with Grandma and Gramps, I had to admit I'd miss Mom and Dad a tiny bit.

Grandma held the screen door open. "Alex," she called as I lugged my bag up the stairs. "About the rooms . . ."

"What?" I asked. I remembered how she'd said one was *a teeny tiny bit nicer*. With Grandma, that could mean anything.

"Never mind," she said.

When I reached the top of the stairs, I walked over to the room on the left and looked inside.

"Wow," I said. The room Sarah had snagged was enormous, with a thick rug on the floor, giant windows in two of the walls, and a huge TV opposite the bed. She was standing by a wooden dresser, unzipping her bag.

She flashed me a grin of triumph. I knew that grin. I had the same one, except I rarely got to use it when Sarah was around. We look so much alike, people think we're twins. But I keep my hair really short, and I never wear jeans—Sarah wears them all the time.

I went to the other end of the hall and pushed the door open. If Sarah's room was a castle, mine was a dungeon. It was dark, small, and filled with boxes. Grandma and Gramps liked to buy weird stuff at auctions and flea markets. I made my way across the room to where a narrow bed was crammed against one wall.

"A teeny tiny bit nicer," I muttered, remembering Grandma's words about Sarah's room. But I didn't plan to spend much time upstairs. I was here to hike in the woods, go fishing, and hang out with my grandparents. I also wanted to explore Thistle's Falls. I'd heard there was an awesome ice cream place in town.

I dropped my duffle bag next to the bed.

That's when I felt the itch.

It started as a tickle, like one ant had crawled up my wrist to the middle of my forearm. But it swelled from ant to spider to tarantula, and then to rat or maybe even a wolverine. I looked at my arm.

What I saw was so horrible, I let out a shout.

TWO

There was a rash on my arm, right below my wrist. No—calling the horrible thing I was staring at *a rash* was like calling the ocean a puddle. This was one monster of a rash. It was as wide as my arm and nearly reached to my elbow. It was red and purple and lumpy, and it looked like it was about to start dripping things I didn't want to see dripping out of my body.

That's a very long description of something I looked at for less than a second before I let out that shout and raced downstairs.

I flung open the screen door and scrambled onto the porch. Grandma was still outside.

I slid to a halt when I realized why she was there. She was talking to Mom, who was standing right at the bottom of the porch steps.

Mom had come back!

She does that a lot. I could see that Dad was waiting for her in the car. This was the worst possible time for Mom to be here. I clasped my hands behind my back to hide my arm.

"What's wrong?" Mom asked. "You screamed."

If she saw the rash, she'd take me right home. No hikes. No fishing. No ice cream. "I saw a spider," I said. "A big one. Huge! Enormous! Big enough to eat a bird!"

As I spoke, I heard Sarah come down the stairs behind me.

Mom frowned like she didn't believe me. I should know better than to try to fool her. Especially when my brain was still trying to get back down from which-ever corner of my skull it had fled to when I saw the rash. I think the part about the bird might have been a bit too much.

Mom held her hand out. "Let me see your arms."

Was I that obvious? I guess I was.

I unclasped my hands, which had built up a layer of sweat, and held my arms out in front of me, palms down.

"Turn your arms over," Mom said.

I turned my arms over.

Mom stared. I stared.

My arms looked perfectly normal. The rash was gone.

"Alex will be just fine. Stop worrying," Grandma said to Mom. A minute later, Mom and Dad finally drove off.

"What was that all about?" Grandma asked after the car reached the end of the driveway and turned onto the main road.

"I'm allergic to something in that room," I said. "We have to switch."

"Yeah, right," Sarah said. "Nice try."

"I am. Come on, I'll show you." I walked up the stairs. I didn't like the idea of getting another rash, but I figured it was better to do it now, so I could change rooms, than to have it happen when I went to bed. I walked into the room and waited for the itch.

Nothing.

I stared at my arms, waiting for the first ant tickle.

No ant. Not even a flea.

Sarah knelt and opened one of the boxes. "Cool," she said, lifting out a pair of wind-up chattering teeth.

"A novelty shop went out of business," Grandma told her. "We bought a lot of their inventory."

At least I'll have something interesting to look at, I thought. Though boxes of jokes and pranks didn't seem anywhere near as good as a giant TV.

Sarah got up. "I guess I'll go unpack my stuff in *my room*." She headed down the hall.

Grandma put *THE BOX* down on a small desk next to the bed.

"Can I look through this stuff?" I asked.

"Sure," she said. "Have a ball."

I opened the closest box, which was barely big enough for a small pair of shoes.

"Yikes!"

There was a bloody hand in the box. I jumped back and tripped over the box behind me, landing on my butt.

"Relax," Grandma said. "That's not real."

"I knew that," I said as I climbed back to my feet. Though it sure *looked* real. "It just startled me." A smile spread across my face as a thought hit me. What if I stuck the fake hand under Sarah's sheets?

Grandma stared right at me. "Don't even think about it," she said.

"How did you know what I was thinking?" I asked.

"Because you're just like your mother," she said.

"No way." I shook my head. I couldn't picture my mom playing jokes on anyone.

Grandma laughed. "Why don't you go run around outside and burn off some of that energy?"

That sounded like a good idea. I grabbed my ball and glove, and went down the hall. "Did you bring your glove?" I asked Sarah. We both loved sports. And we were both left-handed. But that was absolutely all we had in common.

"You bet," she said. "Just give me a minute to finish up."

It looked like she was already unpacked—her bag was empty. But I guess she had more to do. "I'll meet you outside," I said.

It took Sarah a while to come down, but I passed the time throwing pop-ups to myself and watching the squirrels chase each other around the front yard. They were dashing across the grass, skittering up trees, and leaping from branch to branch like acrobats. It looked like their grandma had told them to burn off some energy, too.

"Hey," Sarah said when she joined me, "if you really were allergic, I'd have swapped rooms with you."

"I know."

"Here," she held out a stick of gum.

"Thanks." I unwrapped the gum, which promised MASSIVE BERRY FLAVOR, and popped it in my mouth. By about the second or third chew, I knew something was wrong.

My mouth tasted like fish—and not good fish. Not even bad fish. This was definitely terrible fish.

"BLEH!" I spat out the gum.

Sarah was laughing so hard, she was folded over like she had a stomach virus.

"What's so funny?" I asked.

She couldn't even speak. She handed me the pack of gum. Each stick was labeled with BERRY FLAVOR, but the outside

of the package read: DOCTOR QUACK-WACKIE'S PRANKSTER GUM. IT TASTES LIKE DEAD FISH!

Well, that was sure true. "You got that gum from a box in my room, didn't you?" So that's what she was doing upstairs.

"Guilty," Sarah said.

"I'll get you back," I said.

"I'm sure you will," she said. But her grin hinted that she wasn't worried.

After we'd played catch for a while, we sat on the porch steps and watched the squirrels. Then we went back inside.

"Want to help Grandma and Gramps make dinner?" Sarah asked.

"I need to unpack," I said.

What I really needed was to check the boxes for a good joke to pull on Sarah. I went up to my room, but the boxes were gone. So I went downstairs, where my grandparents were peeling potatoes and chopping onions.

"What happened to the boxes?" I asked.

"We took them to the attic," Gramps said. "Feel free to look through them up there. They have some wild stuff. Great pranks. All sorts of fun things!"

"I think I will," I said.

I went up the stairs and heard Sarah following behind me before I even reached the second floor. I guess she knew what I was planning. I'd just have to figure out a way to be sneaky. The problem was, I'm not a sneak.

As we climbed the attic stairs, my arms started to itch.

"Oh, no," I said. I didn't want another of those monster rashes. But I also didn't want to let Sarah spend time alone with a ton of pranks. Maybe I could put some anti–itch lotion on my arms. It was worth a try. I certainly had just about every type of allergy cream there was, thanks to Mom. I went back down to my bedroom and reached in *THE BOX* to sort through the tubes and bottles. But the itching had stopped.

Weird. I headed back up the stairs and my arms started to itch again. I decided to ignore it. Even if the rash came back, and even if it was terrible to look at, it seemed to go away just as quickly as it appeared. I wasn't going to let allergies run my life.

I climbed all the way up the stairs, crossed the landing, and opened the attic door.

"Aaaahhhhhhhhhhh!!!!!!!!!!!!!!!!!!!!!" Sarah screamed, thrusting a bloody hand in my face.

I shouted and jumped back. "Very

funny," I said after I got control of my heartbeat.

"Got you!" Sarah said as I walked through the door and knelt by the closest box. "I love this stuff."

I wasn't listening. My arms were itching so badly, I figured I'd have to leave the attic. It was even worse than before. And the rash was on both arms now. I was afraid Sarah would make fun of me, but she was already opening another box.

This isn't worth it, I thought. I decided to leave.

"Look," Sarah said, holding up a large metal can painted bright orange and covered with black lettering. "It's Doctor Quackwackie's Patented Vanishing Powder. It says it makes stains, spots, and spills disappear like magic. That's perfect for you!" She pulled open the lid and walked toward me. "I'll make you vanish, and I can have the grandparents all to myself."

"Stop it!" I knocked the can from her hands. Powder went flying all over, getting in our hair and eyes and noses. Neither of us vanished. Sarah let out a monster sneeze so fierce, she bent over. This time, at least, she wasn't laughing at me, and my mouth wasn't filled with the taste of dead fish.

I didn't sneeze. Instead, I let out a gasp. There was someone standing in front of me, in the cloud of powder! But the only way I knew he was there was because he wasn't there. I mean—there was a person-shaped adult-size powder-coated spooky emptiness in the dust reaching toward me. As I stared and rubbed my eyes, the emptiness filled in with a few transparent details, like someone was tinting a sketch with light dabs of watercolors. He was thin and tall, wearing a strange hat that looked like only a brim—a type of visor, I guess—and clothes like the kind you would see in ancient photos from the eighteen hundreds.

There's only one kind of person who looks like he isn't there . . .

"Ghost!" I shouted.

THREE

Sarah had recovered from her sneeze. But she was still bent down, reaching for the can of powder. "Ha-ha. Very funny," she said, not looking up. "Nice try, but you'll have to do better."

Then she looked up.

Sarah screamed. I grabbed her shoulder and dragged her toward the door. Halfway there, she started moving on her own. We both shot for the stairs. I looked over my shoulder on the way down, but nothing was following us.

We didn't say anything more until we

got to the bottom of the stairs. My heart was pounding so hard, I could hear it.

"Was that . . . ?" Sarah said.

"Did we really . . . ?" I said.

"It couldn't be . . ." Sarah said.

"It had to be . . ." I said.

"Maybe we didn't see what we thought we saw," Sarah said.

"There's a lot of stuff crammed in the attic," I said. "Maybe it was a mannequin or a reflection in a mirror."

"Or a painting," Sarah said.

I knew neither of us sounded very convincing. But a tiny part of my brain was already doubting I'd really seen a ghost.

"We need to go back, to make sure," Sarah said.

"No way," I said. I checked my arms. The blotches had faded away. That was weird.

"Come on. We'll go up. We'll turn on all the lights. We'll look all around," she said. "Maybe we'll figure out what we really saw. Then we can stop worrying."

"Okay." I definitely didn't want to go back to the attic. But if she was brave enough to suggest we go do it, I had to be brave enough to go along with her. And she was right—if we found an explanation for what we'd seen, we could relax. It would be terrible to spend the week wondering what I'd run into every time I turned a corner or walked through a doorway.

We went up the steps. I expected my arms to itch again, but they didn't. We found the switches and turned on both ceiling lights. And we each grabbed a flashlight from a box marked EMERGENCY SUPPLIES. We checked every inch of the attic. There was nothing that could be mistaken for a ghost, even if your eyes were dusted with vanishing powder.

"Maybe it was real," Sarah said. "But why isn't it still here?"

"I think we scared it off," I said.

"You can't scare a ghost," she said.

"How do you know?" I asked.

She opened her mouth. And then she shut it.

"We don't know *anything* about ghosts," I said.

"I guess you're right."

I backed away from the attic. "Let's go outside." I wanted to be in a place where a ghost couldn't sneak up on us.

"Were you two wrestling?" Grandma asked as we walked past her on our way through the kitchen.

"We were playing ghost tag," I said.

When we got outside, we walked across the field in back toward the little creek that cuts through the property. My arms started to itch a bit more.

I thought about how they'd itched when I first went into the bedroom and into the attic. And later, they didn't itch, even when I went back to the same spot. An idea—a crazy, unbelievable, amazing, astounding, ridiculous idea—trickled into my mind.

"Sarah?"

"Yeah?"

"This is going to sound totally crazy, so promise you won't laugh," I said.

"I might never laugh again," she said. "What do you want to tell me?"

"I think I might be allergic to ghosts," I said.

To my relief, Sarah didn't laugh.

"I think the ghost might have been in my bedroom when I went there the first time," I said, "and then it wandered up to the attic when we all went to the bedroom. Maybe it doesn't like crowds. I think *it* was giving me the rash."

"And you're not itching at all now?" Sarah asked.

"I wasn't," I said. "Until we got near the middle of the field. I think the itch is getting worse again."

As I stared at the small blotches that dotted my skin, Sarah said, "That's it!"

"What's it?" I asked.

"You're like a tracker," she said. "The itch is a signal. If we see where it gets weaker or stronger, maybe we can find the strongest spot and find the ghost and see if that's what it really is."

At first, I was going to tell her that that was a ridiculous idea, but after I thought about it, I realized she was right. That still left one question: "Do we really want to find it?" I asked. I glanced back at the house. It did sort of look creepy and spooky. So did the woods off in the distance, far beyond the creek.

"It could be something else you're allergic to that moves around, like a bird or a mouse," she said. "It would be good to find out for sure."

"But if it *is* a ghost, I don't want to find it," I said. "Especially if I'm allergic to it."

"Would you rather have it find us?" Sarah asked.

"I'm not all that thrilled with either of those choices," I said.

She put a hand on my back and pushed

me toward the creek. "Come on. It will be fun. Like a video game. Hold your arms up where I can see them. Wow, that really is an ugly rash."

We crossed the stream at a shallow spot, stepping on rocks so our sneakers wouldn't get too wet. The rash grew larger and itchier. Sarah's idea was working. Then after we'd walked a little farther, the rash started to fade. That was good, because I had a hard time keeping myself from scratching it.

"We're moving away from the ghost. Try going left," Sarah said.

I did. The rash faded more.

"It has to be to the right," she said.

I turned and realized I was facing an old barn. Sure enough, as I walked closer, the rash grew larger and darker. And itchier. *Please be a bird,* I thought. *Please be a bird, please be a bird, please be a bird . . .*

"He's in there," Sarah said when we reached the barn door.

"No kidding." My arms were well past tarantula again and on their way to bobcat. I gave both arms a couple small scratches.

We went inside the barn. It was empty, except for an old tractor and some rusted hand tools. No ghost. I would be really happy to spot a mouse right now. Or anything else I couldn't see through.

Sarah pointed to a ladder that led to the hayloft. "We have to check up there."

"I guess." I followed Sarah up the ladder.

The ghost was there. He seemed even clearer now, though he still wasn't solid. I could make out the small buttons on his shirt, the larger ones on the vest he wore over it, and the tufts of hair that were trapped by the strap of his visor.

He drifted toward me.

I shouted.

Sarah screamed.

The ghost fled over to the far wall. And then he paused, as if leaving the shelter of the barn scared him. A moment later, he went right through the wall.

"Nice going," Sarah said. "You scared him off."

"I thought you didn't believe ghosts could be scared," I said.

"I changed my mind when I saw you scare it," she said.

"Me?" I said.

"Yeah, you," she said, "with that high-pitched scream of yours."

"I didn't scream," I said. "I shouted."

"You screamed," she said.

"No I didn't. And your scream is a lot louder and higher than mine," I said.

"No it isn't."

"Yes it is," I said.

"Is not," she said.

I was about to reply "Is, too," when I noticed my rash was gone. Now there was no doubt in my mind—I was definitely allergic to ghosts. Or at least to this ghost.

Unfortunately, I knew there was nothing in *THE BOX* for a ghost allergy. I took a closer look at my arms. They were still a bit blotchy. Maybe the ghost hadn't gone far away.

"Now what?" I asked.

"We need to think about this," Sarah said.

"But not here," I said. Even though the ghost was gone, the barn was still dark and kind of creepy.

"Let's go to Gramps's studio," Sarah said. "I want to check it out, anyhow."

We walked to the garage, right next to the house. I watched my arms the whole time, but the faint blotches never changed. There was a room upstairs where Gramps did his drawing. It had all sorts of paintings and sketches on the walls and a suit of armor in one corner.

I'd just picked up the latest copy of *Little Grendella* from a bookcase next to Gramps's drawing table when my arms started to itch.

The ghost came right through the wall. He moved toward me. A shout rushed from my lungs to my throat.

A hand clamped over my lips.

"Mmmmffff!" My cheeks almost exploded as my shout got trapped inside my mouth. But this time, the ghost didn't flee.

Instead, he reached out, like we were playing ghost tag—for real. Sarah screamed right in my ear. The ghost didn't seem to be bothered by that.

He put his finger on my arm. My skin felt like it was on fire. Sarah clamped her hand harder across my mouth.

My arms were dark purple now. I was afraid my flesh would fall from my bones. I tried to pull free from Sarah so I could race away and stop the pain.

"No!" Sarah said. "Wait! Look!"

She unclamped my mouth and pointed at my arm. Her eyes grew wider in amazement.

I looked, and my own eyes grew wide. And, naturally, I let out a shout. Or maybe it was a scream.

FOUR

Something was written on my left arm, as if part of the rash had been wiped away by the ghost's finger.

THISTLE

I checked my other arm. There was a message on it, too.

PLEASE HELP

Both arms were bathed in an itch so fierce it felt like I'd tried to embrace a bonfire. I'd never felt anything even halfway as bad as this. And I'd had some legendary wipeouts on bikes, skates, and scooters.

I turned toward the stairs. I knew the pain would vanish as soon as I moved away

from the ghost. But before I even took a step, the itch had already started to fade.

I looked back up at the ghost. It was fleeing again. And just like in the barn, it paused by the wall, as if it really didn't want to leave the garage. But then it leaped through the wall and was gone.

"You scared it off," Sarah said. "You really need to learn to control that horrible scream of yours."

"It's NOT a . . ." I sighed and let it go. Maybe my shout was a little bit scream-ish. But not a whole lot. "Never mind. At least we have a message."

I watched the words disappear as the rash around them grew fainter. But the rash didn't completely fade. It looked a bit redder and larger than when we'd entered the studio.

"But what does the message mean?" Sarah asked.

"It's about the town," I said. "I think we need to do something in Thistle's Falls to help the ghost."

"If we want to help the ghost," Sarah said.

"We sort of have to," I said. "Otherwise, it might keep showing up and making me itchy."

"So *we* don't have to help the ghost," Sarah said. "*I'm* not getting itchy."

I stared at her. She laughed. "I'm kidding. There's no way I'd miss out on this."

"Thanks," I said. "I wonder what we have to do."

"We won't know that until we figure out what the message means," Sarah said. "Wait!" she grabbed my arm.

"Ouch! Let go."

She let go. Then she told me her idea. "We don't need to guess about the message. We can track the ghost down again and ask for more information."

"No!" I was absolutely not going to suffer through another round of rash writing. "We'll go into town and figure this out."

"Sure. We'll try that first." Sarah looked at her watch. "It's almost time for dinner. We can go into town tomorrow."

As if on cue, we heard a ding-a-ling-a-ling sound from outside. When we left the garage, I saw Gramps on the porch, ringing a triangle.

"I found it in the kitchen," he said. "In the old days, they used these to call the farmhands in for supper. There are lots of interesting old things all over the house."

"That's for sure," I said, letting out a quiet sigh.

Sarah sniffed the air. "Something smells great."

That was sure true, too. Dinner was awesome. Our grandparents wanted to have a special "welcome to our new home" meal to celebrate the move. Grandma had cooked up a pot of her famous tomato soup. Gramps fried up a batch of his hand-made pierogis, which are little pockets of pasta stuffed with mashed potatoes. I feel that any dinner where you get pasta *and* potatoes is a great dinner. There were plenty of vegetables, too. I usually don't like broccoli, but Grandma had roasted it in the oven and it was delicious.

In the middle of dinner, my arms started prickling, and I caught a flicker of motion by the doorway that led from the kitchen to the hall. The ghost was there. I looked at Sarah. She saw it. I watched Grandma and Gramps. Neither of them seemed to see it. I guess when

you got vanishing powder in your eyes and also got it on something that was already vanished, strange things happened.

The ghost drifted closer. The itching grew worse. It was

time to test Sarah's theory. I let out a scream.

The ghost backed off. But he didn't flee as quickly as before. I think he was getting used to my scream. Grandma and Gramps leaped from their chairs.

"What's wrong?" they both asked.

"I saw a mouse!" I said. I pointed at the floor.

"If mice make you scream, you're going to lose your voice this week, and we're going to lose our hearing," Grandma said.

"This is the country," Gramps said. "You can't *not* see mice. They're everywhere."

"Sorry," I said. I glanced toward the doorway. The ghost was gone. *For now.* I checked my arms. They were a little blotchy. I didn't think my grandparents would notice, yet. But if the blotches got much worse, they'd see them for sure. And maybe tell Mom. Even worse—what if they saw the fully formed monster rashes? They would totally panic.

I tried not to worry about all of this as I finished my food.

"I can't believe it," I whispered to Sarah when we were clearing the table after dinner.

"About the ghost?" she whispered back.

"No. About the broccoli. It was great." I'd even had a second helping. I mean, the ghost was hard to believe, but me liking broccoli was truly amazing.

After dessert—did I mention there were two kinds of pie?—we played board games until everyone started to get sleepy.

"Guess I'll go watch a little television," Sarah said after we'd put away the games. "Actually, I think I'll watch a *big* television." She flashed me a grin.

"It's not hooked up," Grandma said. "No cable. No satellite. No broadcast. Sorry."

It was my turn to flash Sarah a grin. Though I knew, no matter how much she might tease me, if the TV worked, she'd share. She might like to make me suffer a bit, or a lot, but she wasn't selfish.

"At least I brought my phone," she said.

"No signal for that, either," Gramps said. "We do have a landline if you want to call your folks later."

Sarah and I looked at each other. No TV. No Internet. Where were we?

Both grandparents pointed to a bookcase. "There's your entertainment," Gramps said.

I went over and studied my choices. There were lots of books about monsters. No thanks. I'd had enough supernatural creatures for one day. There was a thick book about ghosts. Sarah grabbed that.

"Try this one," Gramps said, handing me a book called *Treasure Island*. "I loved that story when I was your age. Still do."

"Thanks." The cover looked pretty cool, with promises of pirates. I took the book upstairs and got ready for bed. Then I started reading.

Gramps was right. *Treasure Island* was an exciting story. But after a long car ride, a day spent running around outside, and a belly full of a little too much dinner and a lot too much pie, I was half-asleep before the end of chapter one.

As I put the book on the desk and turned off the lamp, I felt the last thing I'd want to feel alone, upstairs, in the dark.

My arms started to itch.

FIVE

I didn't need to turn on my light. The ghost was lit with a soft glow. No. That's not right. No light spread from him. But I could see him as if the lights were on. I guess the ghost wasn't the only one who was getting used to things that frightened him. I was still sort of scared, but I wasn't terrified.

He reached out a hand. Was he going to leave another message on my arms?

"Your messages hurt me. They hurt a lot," I said, scrunching away from him.

He paused, but he didn't back off. Then he started to reach out again.

"I'm only a kid," I said. "It's bedtime. I can't go running around right now, trying to help you. I'd get stopped by the first adult who saw me. If you want Sarah and me to help, wait until morning. Okay?"

This time, the ghost backed away. I guess he understood me. *Great*, I thought as he passed through the wall. *Now I'll never get to sleep.*

But to my surprise, the next thing I knew, it was morning. I checked my arms. The blotches had faded a lot, but they were hard to miss.

My grandparents let me help make breakfast. I like to cook, and I especially love making French toast. The only tricky part was that I kept having to shift and turn as we moved around the kitchen so they wouldn't notice my arms. I would

have put on a long-sleeve shirt, but I didn't bring any.

Right after we started eating, I felt that too-familiar itch. I looked past Sarah, at the bottom of the steps. The ghost was there, moving toward me. The rash started to blossom.

"I'll help!" I shouted at it. "I already said I would!"

Oops.

Everyone turned toward me. I felt my face flush as I stared down at my plate. Afraid to look up, I searched my mind for a way to explain my outburst.

"Thanks," Sarah said to me. "I knew I could count on you." She turned toward our grandparents. "I need to do research on local ghosts. Our newspaper back home publishes stories kids write about their vacations. I asked Alex for help, and he told me he needed to think about it. I guess he made up his mind."

Grandma and Gramps exchanged glances and then shrugged. I was happy Sarah had explained my shout. And I was happy the ghost had backed off.

"Yeah, it will be fun to go into town," I said. "Who knows what we'll discover?"

So, right after breakfast, Sarah and I got our bikes and pedaled down the road toward Thistle's Falls. From what I'd seen online before I left home, the main part of town was about five blocks long, filled with shops of all sorts. There were also some businesses on the side streets. I'd planned to visit the ice cream shop, the toy store—which had a lot of board games—and the kite shop. But all of that would have to wait until I solved my itchy problem.

There was a big banner stretched across Main Street right at the start of town. It read: CELEBRATE THISTLE DAYS!

"That could be fun," Sarah said.

"Right. But I think this will be our first stop." I pointed to a small building in the

middle of the block. I pedaled across the street and coasted my bike to the curb by the Thistle's Falls Historical Society, right between The First National Bank of Thistle's Falls and a coffee shop called Drips and Drops.

I expected the historical society to be a dim, dusty place, sort of like my current bedroom. But it looked a lot like the school library, with big wooden tables, lots of bookshelves, and plenty of sunlight streaming in from large windows.

"Can I help you?" the man behind the information desk asked. A nameplate on his desk read: MORTON HOLWORTH.

"We're trying to learn about local ghost stories." I said. I was half afraid he'd laugh at me. But his body jolted a tiny bit, like he'd been waiting for someone to push his START button.

"Excellent! We have a whole section dedicated to that. Follow me." Mr. Holworth dashed to a file cabinet at the other end of the room and pulled open a drawer.

"Here we go. This is a good start. It's newspaper and magazine clippings." He handed me a thick folder. "That should keep you busy for a while. If you need more sources, we have several books dedicated to our ghosts and many others that mention them."

I sat at a table and slid half the material to Sarah. "Let's split it up. Look for anyone who sounds like"—I glanced over my shoulder, to make sure the man wasn't close enough to hear me, then whispered—"our ghost."

Apparently, Thistle's Falls was a good place to live if you wanted to hang around and haunt people. There was no shortage of ghost stories connected to the town. There were railroad brakemen ghosts, tragic romance ghosts, stranded pioneer ghosts, and pretty much every other kind of ghost you could imagine. Except for my ghost with the vest and the visor.

"I didn't find anything," I said to Sarah after I looked at the last article.

"Same here," she said. "Think we should go through the books?"

"Later. I think we need to build up our strength with some ice cream," I said.

"I like the way you think, cousin," Sarah said.

I got up and handed the folder back to Mr. Holworth. "Thanks."

"Leaving?" he asked.

"Yeah."

"Come back if you have any more questions!" he said. "I don't get a lot of visitors."

"We will." I headed for the door.

"I looked up the ice cream store before I left home," Sarah said. "It sounds great."

"So did I." I guess that was another thing we had in common. I pushed open the door and found myself face-to-flank with a horse. I slid to a halt as the horse's tail swished past my nose.

"Oh my!" Sarah said, as she stumbled into me.

"Run!" I said.

It wasn't just one man on a horse. It was six of them. And it looked like they were robbing the bank!

SIX

The horses blocked us from our bikes. The men, who wore handkerchiefs tied around their mouths to hide their faces, dismounted and charged into the bank.

"This way!" I grabbed Sarah's hand and ran in the other direction, away from the bank, toward an alley. We could hide there until the police came.

"Wait," Sarah said. She tugged at my hand, pulling me to a stop.

"Are you out of your mind?" I asked, tugging back. "There's a robbery."

"They don't seem to be concerned," she said, tugging hard enough to make me decide to stop tugging. She pointed across the street, where two policemen were standing by their patrol car, watching the robbers.

Now, I was totally confused.

"I think this is part of the celebration for Thistle Days," Sarah said.

I really hoped she was right, because that meant we weren't in danger. But I also really hoped she was wrong, because that would mean I hadn't been completely panicking about nothing.

Another half dozen men, dressed as an old-time western sheriff and his deputies, ran toward the bank. I noticed there were a lot of people right down the street from us, watching everything.

"I think you're right," I said to Sarah. "This is a historical reenactment." My parents had taken me to see a group of people reenact a Civil War battle last summer. This was a smaller group of reen-actors, but I was a lot closer to the action.

A few minutes later, the lawmen came back out of the bank. They were leading the bad guys, who all had their hands tied.

The spectators whooped and cheered as the bad guys were marched down the street, but the crowd didn't follow the lawmen. They stayed where they were and watched the bank, as if they knew something else was about to happen.

And then someone different came out of the bank. It was a man, tall and thin, wearing a visor and old-fashioned clothes, including a vest. He had a sack in his hands like the kind banks used for cash in movies and cartoons. He crouched, looked both ways, then slinked down the street.

"That looks like him!" I said. "Our ghost."

The crowd booed him. He picked up speed and ran right past us, letting out an evil cackle.

"He's a bank robber," Sarah said.

"We're being haunted by a thief," I said. "And he wants us to help him." If he was a bad person before he became a ghost, what would he do to us if we *didn't* help him?

"Now what?" Sarah asked.

"Ice cream," I said.

"Of course," she said. "But after that, what do we do?"

"I have no idea," I said. We went to the shop and ordered our ice cream. It was hard to choose. The flavors were amazing. I had one scoop of banana-peanut-butter swirl and one of triple-chocolate fudge with nuts, pretzel nuggets, and toffee crunch. Sarah had a scoop of kiwi-mango with cinnamon sugar and a scoop of something called sweet-tea surprise. She said it was great. I took her word for it.

The tables at the ice cream parlor had flyers on them that looked like old-time newspapers, telling all sorts of stories about Thistle's Falls in honor of Thistle Days. I found one with a picture of our ghost and the story of the bank robbery.

"Joshua Thistle, son of town founder, Ishmael Thistle, was a sickly child, prone to nightmares and fevers," I said, reading the first sentence to Sarah.

"The message!" Sarah said. "It's not about the town. It's about a person."

"That makes sense," I said.

"I thought the town was named after the thistle plant," she said.

"Me too," I said. I read the rest of the story out loud. It was written in old-fashioned language, but I understood the basic idea. Joshua Thistle was terrified of many things, including thunder and the outdoors. He'd even flee a room if someone let out a loud, shrill scream. But he was good with numbers and took a job with the bank. During the robbery, he disappeared with the money from the safe, right before the storm of the century struck the town.

"That explains the visor," Sarah said after I'd finished reading. "People who worked with their eyes a lot used to wear them. He was probably staring at numbers all day."

"And plotting crimes," I said. I turned my attention back to my ice cream. All too soon, it was finished. We left the shop and got back on our bikes.

"I'm not helping him," I said as we pedaled to the farmhouse. "He robbed a bank."

"We don't know that," Sarah said.

"What are you talking about?" I asked. "You saw the reenactment."

"Just because you see something in a play doesn't mean it's true," she said. "There are lots of plays where they changed the facts to make the story more interesting. Besides, you have to prove someone is guilty. That's one of the most important things about the law. We learned that in school."

"Innocent until proven guilty?" I said. "Yeah. I remember." Our teacher had also taught us the word *presume*. It means the same as *assume*, so I'm not sure why they need two different words. But basically, everyone is *presumed* to be innocent.

"We can't presume anything," Sarah said. "We have to find out the truth."

I wasn't sure about that. The people in town seemed pretty certain that Joshua Thistle was a robber. "We'll do more research tomorrow," I said. I figured the guy at the historical society would be happy to see us again. And we'd be happy to see the ice cream shop again. There were plenty more flavors I needed to try. Though none of them involved tea.

When we got to the house, Gramps was waiting for us on the porch. As soon as we reached him, he said, "I presume you have a good explanation for what you did."

He didn't look happy. And I had no idea what he was talking about.

SEVEN

I looked at Sarah. Sarah looked at me. We both looked at Gramps. "What did we do?" I asked.

"Follow me." He opened the screen door and went inside. We followed him.

"Notice anything?" he asked.

I looked at the floor. Back home, I was a notorious mud tracker. I didn't mean to be messy. Sometimes, I'd forget to wipe my feet. But it hadn't rained, and the floor was clean.

"I don't see anything," I said.

Something flew past my face. I swiped at it.

"Notice anything buzzing?" Gramps asked.

Now I saw it. There were flies in the hallway. A lot of flies. They were zipping through the air and crawling on the walls. "Flies?" I asked.

"Numerous flies," Gramps said. "Someone left the screen door open."

Sarah and I exchanged another set of glances. I thought back. I was pretty sure we'd closed the door. It wasn't our fault the flies got in. But how could we prove it? I didn't want Gramps to blame me.

"I know they'll be more careful next time," Grandma said as she walked up to us.

BANG!

We all looked over as the screen door popped open.

"What in the world was that?" Gramps asked. He pulled the screen door closed before more flies got in.

I wondered whether the ghost was trying to help us. But my arms didn't itch. I hoped this didn't mean we had another mysterious visitor to deal with.

BANG!

The door popped open again, swinging wide enough to show us two very frisky squirrels who were chasing each other around the porch, bouncing off the walls, tumbling down the steps, and slamming into the screen door hard enough to make it pop open.

"I'm sorry," Gramps said. "I shouldn't have assumed you were guilty."

"That's okay," I said. "It's an easy mistake to make."

"Well, let me make it up to you kids. How about I take you into town for ice cream?" he asked.

"Sure!" Sarah and I shouted. I know we'd just had ice cream, but this was a vacation.

Grandma joined us and we all went to the car. As I was sliding into the back seat,

I whispered to Sarah, "I think we need to try to help the ghost."

"Presumed innocence," she whispered back with just a bit of a smug smile.

I tried a different flavor, this time— almond-butter cookie dough with cherry jam. But I only had one scoop. Sarah had sweet-tea surprise again. She has no imagination.

When we got home, Gramps let us help fix the latch on the screen door so it was safe from being popped open by frisky squirrels.

After dinner, which we had a whole lot later because everyone was pretty full from the ice cream, we played games again.

"You seem worried about something," Grandma said when we were putting away the game pieces.

"Me?" I asked.

"You keep looking over your shoulder, like you expect to see someone standing there," she said.

"It must be the ghost stories," I said. "Sarah and I did a lot of research."

"Well, I hope this doesn't give you nightmares," Gramps said. "If we send you home all jumpy and jittery, your mom will never let you come back. And that would make me sad."

"Me too," I said. "But don't worry. I know those were only stories."

Grandma pointed at my arms. "Is that a rash?"

"I don't think so," I said.

"Well, let's keep an eye on it," she said.

That night, as Sarah and I were walking upstairs, she said, "I've been thinking about it. The ghost is here because something needs to be fixed. He has some kind of unfinished business that he wants help with."

"How do you know?" I asked.

"I read all about it in the book I took from downstairs," she said.

"What kind of business?" I asked.

"Clearing his name," Sarah said. "That's my best guess. That would mean that he didn't steal the money—and his problem is that everyone thinks he stole it. Does that make sense?"

I nodded. "We just have to figure out how to clear it."

"We will," Sarah said.

As I got into bed, I thought about what Gramps had said. He didn't want me to get all jittery and jumpy. I wasn't worried about that. I'd gotten all of my screaming—I mean, shouting—out of me. I was more worried about getting all rashy.

So naturally, right after I turned out the light, my arms started to itch, and the ghost showed up again. I hoped his appearance wasn't going to turn into a nightly event. I really didn't enjoy this spooky version of getting tucked in.

"We want to help," I told him. "We know you were accused of stealing money. And we're pretty sure you didn't steal it. So we have to figure out what happened." I paused to see if he was going to give me any sort of reply. But he just stood there. I guess the only way he could communicate was with the rash writing. I wasn't thrilled about that. But he needed our help, and I needed to get him to go away forever.

I held my arms out. "Can you give me a clue? A really, really, really short one."

He drifted closer to me and reached a finger toward my left arm. I gritted my

teeth and closed my eyes. My arms itched. And then they hurt. And then the pain moved past hurt into places I don't want to describe. Because describing the feeling would remind me of it. I tried to stay still, but when I knew I couldn't hold back my scream any longer, I yanked my arms away.

When I opened my eyes, he'd already backed off. I hoped he'd had time for the whole message. On my arms, I saw two words. *CAVE* on one arm. *FELL* on the other.

That was it? It didn't seem like enough, but it would have to do. Each new message hurt more than the last one. I definitely didn't want to go through this again. *Cave fell* was the last clue I could handle.

First thing the next morning, I told Sarah what had happened.

"So he fell into a cave, or fell while he was in a cave," Sarah said.

"That could have happened any-where," I said.

"I don't think so," Sarah said. " It has to be near here. The book said that ghosts stay close to places that are important to them."

That would definitely make our search a lot easier. "When we find the cave, we'll find the money," I said. "And then we're done. Bye-bye, ghost. And bye-bye, rash, I hope."

"We need more than just the money," Sarah said. "We also need proof that Joshua Thistle didn't steal it. That's how we'll clear his name."

"How are we going to get proof?" I asked.

"We'll worry about that after we find the money," she said.

When we finished breakfast, I told Grandma and Gramps, "We're going to hike around and explore."

"Have fun," Gramps said.

Grandma looked at my arm. "I think your rash is getting worse. Maybe I should call your mother. She knows about these things."

"I'm fine," I said. "Really." I glanced at

my arms. They definitely didn't seem fine. And then, as I looked back at my grand-parents, my right arm started to feel a whole lot less fine. Another word was forming there!

The ghost had sneaked up behind me and reached over my shoulder.

"Gotta go!" I screamed as I leaped from my chair. "I promised Mom I wouldn't sit around inside all day."

As I raced outside, I looked at my arm. *LEDG* was written there. Another clue. I hadn't given the ghost time to finish it, but I still got the message.

I showed the fading message to Sarah when she joined me. "So we know there's a ledge involved," she said.

"That will help." I looked back at the house. "They must think I'm totally weird. Were they worried when I ran out?"

"They both laughed," Sarah told me. "Then Grandma said, 'That boy is just like his mother.'"

I wasn't sure whether to be relieved or worried. I turned my attention back to our task. "So, somewhere there's a cave with a ledge, or below a ledge, or near a ledge, with a bag of money and an explanation for Joshua Thistle's disappearance," I said.

"If he ended up in a cave around here, we know he didn't run off," Sarah said.

"And we know he became a ghost," I said.

"He must have had an accident," Sarah said. "That's the only reason he wouldn't have returned the money."

"That has to be it. Maybe he fell off a ledge and ended up at a cave."

"We need to find a cave and a cliff," Sarah said.

We started searching for a cliff that had a cave in it. Or beneath it. There didn't seem to be any cliffs. There were plenty of hills. None of them had a cave.

An hour later, we stopped, dropped to a seat on a fallen log, and faced each other. We'd only covered a fraction of the property, but we were hot, sweaty, and thirsty.

"This will never work," I said. It was one thing to decide to search fields and woods for a cave in a cliff. It was a completely different thing to actually find anything. "It was a bad idea to try to do this on foot."

"There's too much land," Sarah said. "It's like a needle in a haystack."

"Or a needle in a stack of haystacks," I said. "I wish the ghost could draw a map." I glanced down at my arm and pictured a whole map there. "On second thought, I don't want a map." And I really didn't want to tell the ghost that we'd failed. Another brush or two with him and my arms would be so bad Grandma wouldn't call Mom—she'd put me in the car and drive me to Mom. Or the hospital.

Sarah popped up as if she'd been startled by a ghost. Before I could ask her what was wrong, she grabbed my shoulder and shouted, "That's it! I know what we can do!"

EIGHT

"We need a topographical map," Sarah said.

"What's that?" I asked.

"It shows elevation," she said. "You know, how high or low stuff is. So we'll see cliffs and valleys. I'm sure Joshua Thistle had some sort of accident. We'll look for a cliff or deep pit where a person wandering in a storm could have fallen. We'll find the cliff first and then look for the cave."

"I'll bet they'd have one of those maps at the historical society," I said.

"And I'll bet Mr. Holworth would be happy for another visit," Sarah said.

So we grabbed our bikes and pedaled back to town.

When we asked about maps, Mr. Holworth was so excited you'd have thought we'd asked to see pictures of his dog.

"I love maps," he said after he brought an enormous book over to our table and flipped it open to the page that covered Thistle's Falls.

"Me too," Sarah said. "I think I want to be a cartographer when I grow up."

She explained to me how to read the map. It was pretty simple. The lines on it showed everything that was the same height. There'd be a new line for every ten or fifty or one hundred feet, depending on the scale of the map. The closer the lines, the steeper the drop.

We looked all over my grandparents' property, but didn't see any cliffs. I scratched my arms, even though they didn't itch. I guess I was getting ready for my next encounter with the ghost.

I got up and walked over to a display case with items from the bank robbery. There was an old book there, open to a page of handwritten numbers. I read the description on the card next to it.

Replica of a typical bank ledger of the sort

that was stolen by Joshua Thistle. The one he took was never recovered. For this reason, nobody knows exactly how much money was stolen. And nobody can explain why he took the ledger.

"Sarah!" I waved her over and pointed at the display. "What if the ghost's unfinished clue wasn't *ledge*? What if it was *ledger*?"

"Then it's not about the ledge of a cave," she said. "It's about a ledger book hidden in a cave!"

"That's great," I said.

"But it doesn't narrow things down," she said. "Even if we know there's a ledger in a cave, the cave could still be anywhere."

"Unless you're right about the accident," I said. "And you have to be. Otherwise, we have no idea what to do."

I went back to take another look at the map, even though we hadn't found any cliffs on the farm. Maybe Joshua Thistle had run into some other kind of danger as he fled from the bank.

Mr. Holworth came to the table and looked over our shoulders. "What are you trying to find?" he asked.

"Our grandparents bought a house just outside of town," I said. "We're looking at the property."

"The Higgins' farm?" he asked. "I heard that had been sold."

"I guess," Sarah said. She pointed to a spot on the map. "The house is here."

"Yup. That's the Higgins' property. Used to be a lot larger. But they sold a big parcel of the land way back in the 1950s. Before then, the property went all the way to here." He tapped a spot on the map much farther out than the hills. "Way back, one of the Higgins was pals with Joshua Thistle."

Sarah's mouth opened, like she was about to say something. I could tell she was excited. I could also tell she didn't want to talk to me until Mr. Holworth left. Luckily, the mail carrier came in just then with a package. As soon as Mr. Holworth walked over to the desk, Sarah jabbed a spot on the map with her finger.

"Here," she whispered. "Look at the drop. It's super steep. See how it's right in line with where the road out of town curves? And it's on the path you'd take from the bank to the farm."

I looked where she pointed. There was definitely a cliff. If someone had left town in a bad storm and didn't follow the curve of the road, they'd end up right at that cliff.

"Let's go," Sarah said. "That's where we'll search."

"Wait," I said. I pictured both of us

falling off a cliff. "If he fell, there's nothing for us to find at the top. Let's go around to the bottom. That will be safer. And that's where we need to search for a cave."

Sarah patted my arm. "I guess once in a while you come up with a good idea."

We used the map to figure out the best way there. We had to leave our bikes by the side of the road and then walk into the woods. But the cliff was easy to spot. When we reached the bottom, I craned my neck back to look at the top. It was about thirty feet above us.

"This should be more like finding a football in a haystack," I said.

"Or maybe just finding a haystack," Sarah said.

We started searching, walking slowly, kicking up leaves when they looked like they covered something.

Sarah spotted it.

"There," she said, pointing to the base of the cliff right next to us. "I think it's some sort of cave."

I knelt and looked inside. The opening was only about two feet wide and three feet tall. It was hard to see anything in the

dark space beyond it. "I don't know if we should go in there."

"He probably didn't go far," Sarah said. "He had no reason to." She knelt next to me and reached in.

I was tempted to yell "Boo!" But I think we were past the point of playing tricks on each other. Instead I said, "Be careful. There could be something sharp."

"Or something flat and smooth," Sarah said. She pulled her hand out, holding an object wrapped in a dirty rag.

"What is it?" I asked.

"Feels like a book," she said. "I think this is oilcloth. That's what they wrapped stuff in back in the old days to keep out water."

Sarah peeled away the cloth. She was right. There was a book inside. It was the size of my school notebooks, with a cover made of leather. Small, neat letters stamped in front read: *Thistle's Falls Savings Bank.* She flipped the cover open and thumbed through the pages. They were filled with entries showing deposits and withdrawals.

"That has to be the ledger!" I felt a tingle of excitement run through my body. I also felt there'd be more in the book than a bunch of numbers. Joshua Thistle had mentioned the ledger for a reason. "Look for the last page with writing."

Sarah started turning pages from the back. "I found it!" she said. She pointed to the top of a page, at a date written in the upper-left corner. "July seventeenth. That's yesterday. The date they reenacted the robbery."

"What did he write?"

Sarah read the first sentence out loud. "I fear this will be my last entry, for I have suffered a terrible injury in my attempt to safeguard the town's money from a fierce band of ruthless robbers."

Joshua Thistle's desperate words, even when read by my cousin, turned my shiver into a tremble. And my tremble grew into a shake that rattled my teeth. But I needed to hear the rest.

"Keep reading," I said.

NINE

Sarah read the rest. Joshua Thistle's words were fancy, flowery, and old-fashioned. It would be easier to tell his story in my own words.

He'd been standing near a window at the back of the general store when he'd heard men plotting to rob the bank. He felt the best thing to do would be to take the money away and put it somewhere safe. He took the ledger, too. He was afraid the robbers would use it to figure out who else to rob by seeing which people were always depositing money. Right after he'd slipped out of the bank with the cash, he'd spotted the robbers riding hard down the main street. He'd run off in the other direction, hoping to get to the safety of his friend's farmhouse. That's when the storm struck. It was a monster of a storm, with torrents of rain and a punishing wind. Lightning struck all around him. He was already terrified by the robbers. Now, with booming thunder and blinding lightning, he was beyond terror, in total panic. But he pulled together all of his courage and kept going.

He'd gotten lost. And then he'd gotten in bad trouble. He'd stumbled over a cliff. I'll never forget, in the middle of all the fancy words, one simple sentence. *My leg is broken*. He'd crawled into the cave and waited for the storm to pass. Then, as the sun broke through the clouds, he'd written his story in the ledger. It was his greatest fear that the townspeople he loved so much

would think he was a thief.

His last words were: *I leave my story here as a testament to my innocence and will now endeavor to seek help, for I fear my strength is draining, and my spark of life will not last much longer without aid.*

And that was it.

It took me awhile to stop shaking. The weather was sunny and warm right now, even in the woods, but I couldn't help seeing myself huddled in a small cave, wet, injured, and terrified, cringing with each bone-rattling boom of thunder. I imagined what it would be like, writing desperate words in a journal and hoping someone would find them so I wouldn't be blamed for something I didn't do.

"So he left the cave," I said.

"But he never reached the farm," Sarah said.

"This proves he wasn't a thief," I said. "We can clear his name."

"We can," Sarah said.

"We should bring the ledger right to town," I said.

"We should," Sarah said.

We looked at each other. I knew what Sarah was thinking. And I'm sure she knew what I was thinking.

It would be wonderful to clear Joshua Thistle's name with the ledger. But it would be wonderful, spectacular, amazing, and unbelievable if we showed up in town with the ledger and the money.

"We need to look," I said.

"We need to look," Sarah said, agreeing with me. "But where?"

I stared at the mouth of the cave and then glanced in the direction of the farm. "Maybe he left the money with the ledger," I said.

"If he didn't, it's out there in the woods somewhere, maybe right next to . . ."

She didn't finish her sentence. She didn't have to. I knew what she was thinking here, too. If the money had been with him when he died, we wouldn't find just the money. It was already bad enough I was seeing ghosts. I didn't want to add a skeleton to my list of spooky experiences. "Let's check the cave first."

"Go ahead," Sarah said.

"Me?" I asked.

"Yeah, you," she said. "I already found the ledger. It's your turn."

"Okay, but I'm not going too far." I knelt and reached inside. I started to feel around.

"Ouch!" I yanked my hand back.

"Are you okay?" Sarah asked.

"Yeah. I just touched the sharp corner of a rock." I said. I reached back inside and felt around more carefully, hoping I'd discover some kind of sack. But there was nothing on the cave floor except for dirt and stones. I crawled a little farther inside, but stopped when my knees reached the mouth of the cave. It was too danger- ous to go any farther.

"No sign of a bag," I said.

"I guess we have to search the woods," Sarah said.

"It looks that way." I started to inch my way back out. My hand landed on the sharp rock again.

Wait a minute!

Mom was always telling me not to make assumptions. And Sarah had reminded me not to presume someone was guilty without evidence. Everyone had assumed Joshua Thistle was a thief. They were wrong. The people who did the reenactment also assumed the money was in a sack. So did Sarah and I. Maybe we were wrong about that, too. I slid my hand past the sharp corner of the rock, along the top surface. It was flat and cool. Like metal.

"What's wrong?" Sarah asked. "Why'd you stop?"

"I think I found it." I reached in with my other hand and felt around for three more corners. Yeah, it was a box, nestled among the dirt and stones. I worked it free and dragged it out of the cave.

"You did it!" Sarah said.

"We did it." I dusted off my hands, got to my feet, and looked down at something that had been lying hidden in the cave since the day Joshua Thistle died. It was a rusted old metal box with a handle on each side. It wasn't a bag, like in the reen-actment. I guess people get history wrong sometimes. Or they change things a bit to make a better story. But that didn't matter right now.

I picked up the box and shook it. "Feels pretty full," I said.

I couldn't get the lid up. But Gramps had tools. Sarah and I had done all of the adventurous parts and had all the fun. Now it was time to get some adults involved.

We hiked back to our bikes and rode to the farmhouse, holding the box between us. I'd tucked the ledger under my shirt.

"Well, you two look like you've been on an adventure," Grandma said when we walked into the house.

"We sure have," I said. "Guess what we discovered?"

"More bouncy squirrels?" Gramps asked.

"Not even close," I said.

"Get comfortable," Sarah said. "We have a story to tell you."

Across the room, far away enough that the itch wasn't too bad, the ghost watched us. Sarah told our grandparents all about Joshua Thistle, and about how we'd found the ledger and the box after we'd figured out he'd had an accident. She told them

everything except for the part about the
ghost.

Gramps got his tools and opened the
box. I held my breath as he pried back
the lid. And then I gasped at what I saw.
The box was filled with money! It was
old-fashioned money, but real bills. I felt
like we'd found a treasure chest.

Sarah and I grinned at each other. If grins could talk, ours would be saying, *We are totally awesome.*

"We should take this right into town," Gramps said.

So we got in the car and headed to Thistle's Falls. As we parked, Grandma said, "I wonder whether we should show this to the mayor or the sheriff?"

"Neither," I said.

Everyone looked at me. "I know the perfect guy to take care of all of this." I pointed at the door of the historical society.

"Well, what brings you back?" Mr. Hol-worth asked when we walked inside.

"You're not going to believe it," I said. "Take a seat."

It was my turn to tell the story. After I

was finished, I saw that I'd made the perfect choice of who to give the ledger and cash box to. Mr. Holworth called the mayor, the sheriff, the town council, and the local reporters. Pretty soon everyone was talking, taking our pictures, congratulating us, and discussing how they'd have to change things for next year's Thistle Days.

"You'll be back, won't you?" Mr. Holworth asked. "You have to come back."

"Of course we will," I said.

"Great," he said. "Next year, you can lead the parade. And I need to get to work writing a new scene for the reenactment."

After the excitement died down, we headed out. "That was quite an adventure," Grandma said.

"We should celebrate with ice cream," Gramps said.

Sarah and I looked at each other. "Maybe tomorrow," we both said. I think we'd had too much of a good thing.

Sarah pointed at my arms and smiled. I looked at them. The blotches were completely gone. "We did it," I said.

"We sure did," she said.

We drove to the house. There was a familiar car in the driveway. It was my parents.

"It's not time to go back, is it?" I asked.

"No. But your folks and Sarah's folks wanted to come out for dinner," Gramps said.

"Great," I said. I didn't want to leave the farm yet, but I guess I really did miss Mom and Dad a bit.

I saw them waiting for us on the porch.

As I ran toward them, my arms started to itch.

Oh no! I looked around. I didn't see the ghost. But there was a blotch on each of my arms. If Mom saw this, she'd definitely take me right home. And that wasn't fair. Sarah and I had a whole lot more exploring to do. And we'd done everything the ghost wanted.

The blotches grew darker and bumpier. I slowed, crouched down, and gritted my teeth. I knew the pain that was coming.

But that didn't matter—I was about to have a much bigger problem than another encounter with unbearable pain. I was heading for a major encounter with an un-stoppable allergy doctor. Up on the porch, Mom called, "Alex, what's wrong? Are you sick? Did you have an allergy attack?"

A word formed on my left arm:

THANK

A word formed on my right arm:

YOU

Both rashes immediately started fading. But Sarah had caught up to me and got a quick glimpse of them before they disappeared.

"You're welcome," I whispered. I was glad we'd helped, but I was even more glad my itchy adventure was over. I hoped I would never meet any other ghosts who made me itch. I was definitely sick of mon-sters.

I went up the porch to get a hug from Mom.

"Oh, Alex," she said, throwing her arms around me. "I missed you so much."

"You're killing me!" I screamed as her arms wrapped around me like a pair of boa constrictors.

But it felt kind of nice.

ITCHING FOR MORE?

Check out a sneak peek of the next

MONSTER ITCH

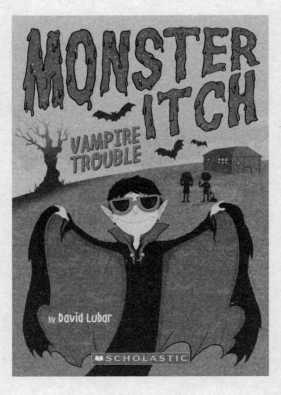

"Strike one," Herbert said from his spot at second base.

"No fooling," I muttered as I pushed myself up from the muck. I could feel my face flushing. If it got any hotter, it would steam off the muddy water that was all over my neck and forehead. After I stepped back to the plate, I glanced at the playground monitor, just to prove to myself that I had to be wrong. Was she really totally uninterested in what had just happened? I'd done a face-first full-body plant in a mud puddle!

But she didn't seem to react at all.

On the next pitch, as I backed up, I felt the itch again, on the third step. As I finished my five steps and started my dash, I felt another sneeze coming.

I gritted my teeth.

I'm not sneezing, I told myself.

I sneezed. This one was even harder. And yeah, I went flying again. And naturally, I landed in the puddle again. But I'd already soaked up most of the mud on my first fall, so this one didn't make things all that much worse.

Still, it seemed to draw even more laughter.

"Strike two," Herbert said.

I had no idea why I kept sneezing. But I realized that maybe this wasn't the time to try for a home run. I'd have plenty of chances to score the three homers I needed.

I sneezed on the fourth step as I backed up. And then I sneezed a second time as I moved forward. But I didn't try to nail the ball— I just sort of lashed my foot out at it and hoped to make contact. I actually made a solid hit. Unfortunately, it was also a weak one, popping up toward second base.

The kickball dropped right into Herbert's hands. I could hear sighs of disappointment from all around the playground as I failed to land in the puddle again. I let out my own sigh because not only was I out, but because, thanks to catching my pop fly, Herbert was up. I was supposed to take his spot on the field, but I was just too muddy and discouraged to keep playing.

"Someone sub for me," I said. I needed to wash off.

As I walked away, the ball smacked the back of my head with a loud POING!

I turned around and instantly spotted the ball's source. Herbert had kicked it right at me.

"Oops, sorry," he said, grinning. "Accident."

"Yeah, right." I didn't believe him. I watched the next pitch so he wouldn't hit me again. Instead, he nailed the ball for a home run. Great. Really totally wonderful and great. I was a mud ball, and Herbert was within one home run of catching me.

I went inside to the art room and used the sink to clean up my face and arms. The art teacher, Mr. Pemberton, had a bunch of old shirts he kept on hand for kids to wear when they painted. He let me borrow one.

I had lunch right after recess.

"What happened to you?" Sarah asked when she saw me walking past the table where she sits with the other girls from the science club. Even with the clean shirt, I was pretty much a mess.

"I sneezed so hard, I flew into a mud puddle," I said.

Sarah laughed. "Wish I'd seen it. That must have been one monster of a sneeze."

As the words left her mouth, her eyes widened. She stared at me. I stared back at her. My eyes widened, too.

"No way," I said. Just the other week, after not having any allergies for a long time, I had gotten a very itchy rash as an allergic reaction to a ghost. But a sneeze wasn't a rash. And there was no ghost on the playground. At least, I was pretty sure Gloomy Girl wasn't a ghost. She wasn't transparent.

But she sure was spooky.

"You're right," Sarah said. "One sneeze doesn't mean anything. Everyone sneezes."

I didn't tell her that it was more than one.

MEET RANGER

A time–traveling golden retriever with search
and-rescue training . . . and a nose for danger

■▲ SCHOLASTIC
scholastic.com